Once Upon a Garden
Doug's Dung

Jo Rooks

MAGINATION PRESS 🍂 WASHINGTON, DC
American Psychological Association

For Mum and Dad, who always encouraged my creativity. —JR

Magination Press
Books for Kids From the
American Psychological Association

Magination Press is a registered trademark of the American
Psychological Association. Order books at maginationpress.org
or call 1-800-374-2721.

Book design by Gwen Grafft

Printed by Lake Book Manufacturing, Inc., Melrose Park, IL

Library of Congress Cataloging-in-Publication Data
Names: Rooks, Jo, author, illustrator.
Title: Doug's dung / by Jo Rooks.
Description: Washington, DC : Magination Press, 2020. | Series:
    [Once upon a garden] | Summary: Doug is teased for not being
    strong, tough, or persistent like the other dung beetles, but
    Belinda the butterfly helps him accept that he has strength in
    a different, wonderful way.
Identifiers: LCCN 2019033323 | ISBN 9781433832376 (hardcover)
Subjects: CYAC: Individuality—Fiction. | Creative ability—
    Fiction. | Dung beetles—Fiction. | Butterflies—Fiction.
Classification: LCC PZ7.1.R66854 Dou 2020 | DDC [E]—dc23
LC record available at https://lccn.loc.gov/2019033323

Manufactured in the United States of America
10 9 8 7 6 5 4 3 2 1

Doug was a dung beetle.

Dung beetles are very strong. Every day,
they practiced lifting, pulling, and pushing
the heaviest balls of dung.

Meanwhile, Doug admired nature.
"Look at these beautiful butterflies!"
called Doug. But no one was interested.

"You need to be **strong**, like this!" said Dan.

"You need to have **power**, like this!" said Doris.

"You must **never** give up, like this!" said Dave.

"You try!" they said.

But even though Doug tried …

and tried …

Doug just couldn't do it.

"You're not strong or powerful.
You've just given up!" they jeered and raced off.

"Don't worry about them," said Belinda.
"You are strong in another way."
And off she flew.

The breeze blew some blossoms through the air ...

and Doug caught a petal in his hand.

Then Doug had an idea.

"What *are* you doing?" smirked Dan.
"Being creative!" said Doug.

Then Doug had another idea.

"What a waste of time," said Doris.
Doug ignored her and just carried on.

Then he had another idea.

And another.

And another!

Doug wanted to show off his work.
"Art? Ha!" scoffed Dave.

Nobody came to see Doug's art. But he couldn't give up on something that made him so happy. He was more **determined** than ever to keep creating beautiful art.

Then he heard a flutter.

"Can I see your art?" said Belinda.

Before long, everyone wanted to see Doug's art.

It made the whole garden smile!
Dave, Doris, and Dan felt very sorry.

"Creativity is your **strength**!" said Dave.
"You have the **power** to make the
whole garden happy!" said Doris.
"And you **never gave up**!" said Dan.

"So, you inspired us to make this!" they said.

"I **love** it!" said Doug.

And since then, Doug has been inspiring
his friends to be more creative ...

and show their **strength**, **power**,
and **resilience** in another way.